TOBA

TOBA

Michael Mark

Illustrated by Neil Waldman

BRADBURY PRESS   SCARSDALE, N.Y.

The author would like to thank *Boundary-2*
and *Young Judaean* for permission
to reprint some of the stories in this volume.

Bradbury Press, Inc.
2 Overhill Road
Scarsdale, N.Y. 10583
An affiliate of Macmillan, Inc.
Collier Macmillan Canada, Inc.
Manufactured in the United States of America
10 9 8 7 6 5 4 3 2 1
The text of this book is set in 14 pt. Garamond.
Library of Congress Cataloging in Publication Data
Mark, Michael, 1957-
Toba.
Summary: Nine stories about ten-year-old Toba and her family,
presenting a picture of Jewish life in Poland around 1910.
[1. Jews—Poland—Fiction.] 2. Poland—Fiction. 3. Family life—Fiction]
I. Waldman, Neil, ill.   II. Title
PZ7.M33927To   1984   [Fic]   83-15679
ISBN 0-02-762300-9

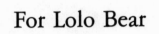

For Lolo Bear

TOOTHACHE

Toba sits deep in her chair, quiet, head bowed. Her shiny curls are dressed in yellow silk bows, scraps from the shawls her Papa sews.

If it were any other day, Toba might very well turn before the mirror and admire her reflection. "Where did you get such locks?" she would hear her Momma say, and she would laugh. But this is not any other day.

The bowl of steaming porridge, thick and lumpy the way she likes it, the way only her Momma makes it, remains uneaten. Toba lets her eyes wander along the pattern of her skirt. It is her favorite skirt, made as most all her clothes are by the skillful hands of her Papa. But still, Toba hated to see it waiting for her on the chair this morning when her Momma called and shook her out of bed. Toba had pretended she was sleeping, afraid to begin the day.

"Be happy your Papa can afford to send you to the dentist," her Momma had warned, pulling the curtains from the window, letting the

dull winter sun disturb the bedroom's darkness.
"You want rotten teeth? Like your Momma?
You want to be ugly?"

Toba had not answered. Words would not be
permitted. She had pouted, hidden beneath
the blanket—also quilted by Papa.

Last night and the night before, she had
awakened, crying from the pain in her mouth.
Her Momma had poured a thimble full of
schnapps onto a piece of cotton, and made her
bite with the sore tooth. The cotton gushed
strong, with a full, hard nut taste. She gagged.
But her Momma clasped one hand under her
jaw and the other over her mouth, keeping
Toba from spitting out the vile swab. After a
quiet moment she had slept.

"Eat your cereal, Toba. It gets cold."

Toba watches her heavy, pale Momma, who
never rests, who is always pouring tea, cutting
loaves, stirring soup, tucking material, brushing
hair—either Toba's or the wavy hair of one of her
two sisters, both blond and older, now at school.

"Eat or wait outside," her Momma's usually
calm voice squawks. She is bent over, poking
the iron into the flaming belly of the black
stove.

Toba knows, before she looks up at the only

4

window in the kitchen, that there is a thick coat of ice on the outside as well as the inside of the glass. She sighs, reaches for the wooden spoon, angles it, and lets it sink slowly into the sea of her breakfast.

The pain began—a prick—nearly a week ago. Toba prayed through the days, during school, walking back home, even as she played, that God should cure her sick tooth or make it die and fall out as her front one had. She did not want to go to the dentist for fear of his metal drill and pliers. She had been to him once before. There was nothing wrong—no pain then. But he had found, or, she thought, had *put* a cavity in her mouth and used his drill.

"When I turn around," her Momma warns from the wash basin, catching Toba playing with her food, "I want your bowl clean."

Toba squints. Her Momma looks oddly small between the cupboards and stove. The kitchen is the largest room in the house they rent from Mr. Polanski, a long, thin man with a short pointed beard who laughs at Toba's every word as if she only tells jokes. Right now, Toba thinks she does not like him.

Toba lifts her spoon laden with cereal and eases it into her mouth. The porridge burns

going down. She quickly follows it with milk.
The sudden cold pains her mouth.

"My darling daughter," her Momma cries,
turning. "So much pain?"

Toba looks at her Momma with earth brown
eyes—her Papa's eyes. Tears spill. Her Momma
sets down the washrag she has held in her right
hand and the long knife in the other, and rushes
to her baby; kneeling, she hugs her.

"Shah. Shah, Toba. It will be all right. Papa
is very proud of you. Shah, shah." She holds
tight and moves Toba to the easy rhythm, her
hushed chant.

Yesterday, upon learning from her Papa that
she would be going to the dentist this morning,
Toba shouted that she refused. He could not
force her.

Toba's Papa, Reb Cohen the tailor, once the
finest dressmaker in Lenchintz—maybe, though
he would never boast of such, in all of Lublin—
is a silent man. His hours, aside from davening
in shul—returning each morning with the other
men of the village before the children's voices
sweeten the air—are passed in his dark workroom, surrounded by needles, threads, materials. He is not a learned man, though he is
familiar with Torah, Talmud and portions of

Kabbala. He is not the scholar he had wanted to be. When he speaks, it is of books, of thought, and of men he respects. If his pockets are not fat with coins, his voice is rich with a deep, hearty tone that charms Toba. And she always knows, by the warmed expressions on their faces, that others, too, are enchanted.

After she had made such an outburst — though she had cut her words short, for she knew she was doing wrong — Toba looked up slowly, shyly to her Papa. His head was lowered, his beard, mostly gray with a few tangled strands of black woven in, lay still on his strong, wide chest. She had not looked to his face for his reaction, her punishment. All was in his hands: only a little larger than her own, white, with curls of fur roaming the backs. Powerful hands, gripping her bony shoulders, than taking her by her thin waist when he was most pleased — holidays, birthdays, special moments for no reason — drawing her to him, his solid bulk.

Each of her Papa's finger tips was fat with padding, as if he had severed the skin, as he would a lining, and filled the insides with cotton. The palms were deeply hollowed, Toba believed, just so her chin could fit so well. She had looked at his hands in the long, loud silence that followed her scream — so shrill it had made her shudder. His fingers were knotted, knuckle wrestling knuckle, red, struggling. The sight forced Toba up to her room, her bed, beneath the blanket, in tears. She was sorry. She would go. She would go. She was sorry.

The next time Toba saw her Papa was at dinner, when she was as silent as he. Unlike other nights, she ignored Anna and Bella — touching and giggling, between eating and cleaning. After the soup, before the meat, her Momma whispered, moistening Toba's ear with warm breath, "Kiss your Papa. Tell him you will be a good girl."

Toba kept her head still, but shifted her eyes to see him, his hands. His arms were folded across his chest. His hands were clenched in fists, almost hidden, like the Gentiles' baby pigs huddling under the momma for milk. She could not bring herself to beg forgiveness.

When she was younger than her ten years, she could ask him to forgive her, though she had never wronged him this severely. She would sing and dance for him, even as he worked, until he would look over, beneath those bushy brows, lighten, and smile at her. That was before his sight had faded, before he went blind. It was not because of his blindness that Toba would not now hug him, strain to fit as much of him as she could between her lithe arms, kiss his scratchy beard over and over, and inhale what she called "Papa's smell." She still did that as often and with as many joyful squeals, though anyone in the family—and those who knew the Cohens well—admitted there was a change, a difference, between the two. It was nothing obvious, barely noticeable, a feeling, an aura—in some ways similar to the subtle glow that rises from a usually sallow-faced girl once she has fallen in love. It was as if father and daughter had traded their most deeply kept secrets, or beheld the same final sight, before, as he put it, "the lights dimmed."

An hour after dinner, a timid Toba came down the steps from her room and sat on the wooden bench—used for that week of shiva they had sat for Tante Jenny, her Papa's sister. She waited for him to call her. But his voice was silent. Toba waited past eight o'clock, two hours later than any other night. She could hear his heavy, steady breaths, and the rustling of material. Brokenhearted, she gave up hope when her Momma said it was time for bed. After changing into her night clothes—the ones with the matching slippers — she washed her face, brushed her teeth, using light, tiny strokes near the troublemaker, and came again to kiss her parents good night.

As on any other night, her Momma handed her the kerosene lamp from the kitchen table, kissed Toba's face (this night it was a worried face), and playfully turned her around and pushed her toward the dark room where her Papa worked.

Toba entered, bringing the yellow glow of light. It took a moment — her lungs lost their breath — before she could say in her sweetest, highest-pitched song, "Good night, Papa."

Again she waited, this time for him to inflate with great breaths, sign contentedly, stick the needle he worked so rapidly, so precisely even in the coldest dark through the material in his hand, place it on the table and spread his arms for her to rush in. But he did not. Toba could see, shining on the table near the spools of thread six needles aligned perfectly in a row, largest to smallest, all eyes, widest to thinnest, empty.

Her Papa kept to his stitching. After a long while, when Toba was not sure if he thought she was still there or not, he nodded. Through his blindness, his closed lids, she knew her Papa could see her tears. She turned and, weighed down by the huge lamp, half tumbled out into the kitchen, where she left the lamp on a chair and ran up to her room.

When she woke, shivering from cold and the throbbing tooth, her tears were not only from the infection. And when she cried out, she cried louder than she had to, loud enough to wake her Papa, knowing he slept deeper. But only the figure of a woman, hair down, silhouetted by the accompanying lamp, came to her bed.

"The tooth, Tobala?"

She nodded and confessed that she had not threaded Papa's needles, that she saw when she went into his room that they all needed to be threaded. But he did not ask her. He would not kiss her good night.

Her Momma had rocked her quiet enough to apply the schnapps to the cotton, the cotton to the tooth, hands firmly to Toba's jaw and mouth.

"It is time, *Tatala*. Put on your warm coat."

Wiping the remaining tears from her cheeks, Toba stands from her chair and walks to the closet where she, on tiptoes, reaches high and pulls her winter coat by its sleeve off the hook. Her mother clears the bowl, spoon, and glass from the table, places them in the basin, turns,

and walks, shaking her hands dry, into her husband's workroom.

Toba stands weakly, praying. If she could only hear her Papa's voice before she goes to the dentist, if she could feel his hands stroke her face. Her Momma emerges, hurrying on her way up the stairs, untying the back of her apron.

Toba feels a sharp pain in her mouth. She does not deserve to hear his voice. Why should he waste his breath on such a bad girl?

"Toba, my needles!"

THE FAIR

"Yes, sir, only five kopeks. It is the finest materials."

Toba smiles her prettiest practiced smile, and strokes the green and brown felt as she does her well-behaved dolls. It is the first Sunday of August, and, as on all first Sundays of the month, Toba and her Momma are at the Litvak Fair, selling her Papa's shawls.

"Yes, sir, I will try it on, but it will look much more beautiful on your wife at home."

Toba—not Anna, not Bella—is the one to go with Momma. Her Papa tells her she is the reason the shawls sell so well. She is also the reason the sky is blue and the sun shines.

By dark, Toba is tired and her stomach aches from hunger. Her throat is raw, and, as always by sundown, her Momma wraps a scarf around her little one's neck. Even on a warm, sticky night such as this, Toba does not complain, but stands still, raising her chin for her Momma's hands to tuck the scarf neatly.

"The best customers come at night," her Momma croons to weary Toba, looking out into the fading field. "The dark hides the bare patches. The stars make the trim sparkle."

Though the weather is clear this Sunday, as it was the Sunday before, it has not brought those nearsighted customers with coins burning holes in their pockets, those women who must have this and that. Many people passed Toba and her Momma's clean blankets spread with shawls; some smiled, some nodded.

"Dig into your purses, misers," her Momma would growl beneath her sour breath. Sometimes, as the people passed and looked, she would raise a shawl to her face and rub her fat cheek in soft circles. But this brought little luck. Today was full of those grumbles, full of her Momma's curses — some so involved that Toba would lose track and forget at whom the sharp words were aimed.

When there is no one to sell to but the still trees, standing stiff as strangers, and the pale half-moon like a broken kopek, Toba's Momma spreads her apron over her heavy knees and counts out their poor earnings, going on about a man ("a toad," she calls him) who promised to return with twelve kopeks to buy three shawls.

It was a fine price, they all agreed—but he was never seen again. "He should have a wife as barren as the land he works."

Carefully, mother and daughter fold and pack the too many leftovers—one large sack for the woman's shoulders and a smaller one for the girl's.

"Maybe Papa should make new shawls, or scarves," Toba offers after a few minutes of trying to keep pace with her Momma up the rocky hill. "Maybe everyone has bought our shawls and now they need scarves." This is a good idea and Toba repeats it sternly, for business is a serious matter.

What else can he do? her Momma answers to herself. *The man is blind. Is it his fault? Is it mine?*

"Maybe," she answers Toba, "you can move your tongue less and your feet more? Save some air for the bear who will eat you if you do not hurry."

Toba frowns. She has heard this before, though sometimes it is the grass, or the ducks, or the chickens who need the air. When it is the butterflies or the birds, it means her Momma is not really angry with her—she just wants Toba to be quiet enough so she can hear her own thoughts. This is Toba's reasoning, something she is proud of. Who can think of floating butterflies

and singing birds, and be angry? It is impossible.

Toba does not believe a bear will eat her, though she has heard stories of big black ones coming out of the woods just to taste the toes and ears of bad little boys and girls. Those are just stories mommas and papas tell to make their children behave. When pigs, weasels, or donkeys need the air she wastes, then she knows it is time to be quiet and tend to her chores, or if those are done, to keep out of the path of her Momma's knife-sharp footsteps.

This week, the donkeys and pigs have needed so much air they could float to the sky. But now it does not bother Toba that her Momma wants silence—she, too, is busy listening to the quiet, faraway voice of wisdom telling her what a goat would mean, or a cow, or a lamb. They pass the villages of Porchtick, Steatle, and Hobra before Toba feels certain that a cat—depending on whether it is a kitten or a stray—would either mean her Momma is in a playful mood or about to strike. Toba looks up with her discovery. What she sees startles her. There is a moment, then another, when she cannot find breath. Then, slowly, as if she were seeing through the smoke of a fire, she realizes that the still, dark figure in the road ahead is not a bear at all, but her Momma.

The more steps Toba takes—at first, small steps with tiny pauses between each—the more her Momma changes: from a big, black bear to a cow with two heads, a deer, a tree. The sack beside her is a sheep, a dog, a rock.

When Toba comes close, she can see in her Momma's hard, shining eyes that something is wrong.

"Do not tell Papa of our day. We did fine. Do you hear?" She speaks in a harsh voice. Toba is about to nod or ask why—she does not know which—but her Momma does not wait for a response. She bends, crooked, slides her shoulders low, and with a grunt, lifts the load onto her back, turns and again starts home.

Toba has trouble regaining her pace. It is as though her Momma's commands add more weight to her bundle. What will she tell Papa when he asks about their day—how many kopeks they brought back? Is it her fault people do not buy the shawls?

Once home, Toba sits at the table, eating her thick potato stew, drinking the cool water.

"Such a day we had! Sixty kopeks! Sixty-five! Such a day!"

Toba listens to her Momma's lies. She knows exactly how many kopeks they made. She has heard her Momma curse each one, some twice, because she had more curses than kopeks.

"Sixty-five! Did you hear the good news, Toba?" her proud Papa asks. "You must have sold hundreds of my rags with each smile."

Toba does not answer. The water in her mouth tastes dirty.

"Tobala, do you hear? Why is my happiness so quiet?"

"She is saving the air," her Momma answers.

"For whom?" her Papa laughs. "For whom are you saving the air, little apple?"

The worms, Toba thinks.

NIGHT

Toba turns once, then again. It is no use. Her soft bed, usually warm and friendly, has suddenly become a stranger, poking and pinching her all over. She would close her eyes and try to go back to sleep, but she is too frightened. Yet if she does not close her eyes, how will she possibly last until the lazy sun rises?

Toba decides to keep her eyes wide, but not look toward her closed bedroom door, which seems to have grown large and crooked. She will also keep away from her clothes closet, where she is almost certain nothing is hiding; still, as her Momma says, "There is no good sense in tempting the fates." So, eyes open, gathering all the light they can hold, Toba forces her thoughts away from her angry bed, itchy night clothes, and whatever might be about to leap from the shadows, back to her dreams.

First there was the busy family of moles, digging deep into the rich soil, who soon turned into goldfish, glimmering beneath the blue waters. After that, Toba's dream grows dim. How did the goldfish become flying birds, resting on the tops of pointed trees?

The answer matters little. The dreams have worked their spell and cast out the fear that made Toba's heart tremble, although she still finds herself not sleepy, or even the least bit tempted by her pillow.

"This is very odd," Toba says aloud to keep herself company. "I'm always a *good* sleeper." Her Momma has said so on many occasions. This past winter, when a wind brought down a nearby row of oaks with a terrible noise, Toba slept through the night without so much as a whimper.

"You are a good sleeper, Toba," her Momma had said.

A proud Toba had gone off to tell Greisha, her schoolmate, who made a joke at Toba's expense. He said, "You are a good sleeper, Toba, because you are only *good* when you are *asleep*."

Toba lets out a laugh, then quickly covers her mouth. If she is the only one awake, she must be very quiet. But there is one problem. The more Toba strains to hush her laughter, the more her laughter grows. She pulls her two blankets over her head and laughs and laughs until she is nothing but a bouncing ball of loose giggles. It is as if the night is tickling her and refuses to stop.

Finally the storm of laughter calms, leaving Toba on her back, beneath the blankets, panting for breath. And here the idea strikes her that being the only one awake in the whole house in the dark of night can become a great adventure.

Again a laugh escapes, for this idea is the most amusing of all.

With a great flurry, as if she'd planned this very moment for weeks, Toba kicks off her blankets, lets fly her pillow, swings over the bed's edge, and lands her feet into their waiting slippers. She ties on her robe — and softly, *softly*, tiptoes to her now quite-funny-looking bedroom door.

In the hallway, barely lifting her slippers from the smooth wooden floors, Toba slides into Anna's bedroom. The room is still. There is only the steady breaths of the heavy sleeper, looking like a small hill rising from her flat bed. Toba moves only a whisper away.

Anna's skin is clean and fresh as cream, everyone says. And they are not liars. Toba lets her finger tips trace her older sister's full cheek, which seems to glow even in the dark.

Anna must dream of sunshine, Toba thinks.

Above all, Anna treasures her time outside, in the garden, tending to the vegetables. Even in winter she takes long walks in the endless drifts of snow.

She must dream of filling her apron with large, red radishes, round white onions, and heavy potatoes, Toba thinks.

Closing her eyes, she places her cheek gently to sleeping Anna's and holds her breath.

Yellow streams of sunlight. Sprays of spring rain. Carrots dancing with stalks of celery. Rolling onions chasing green lettuce down mountains of tiny, white flowers.

This is Anna's dream. Toba is able to see every detail perfectly. She has dreamed Anna's dream.

The world of the night is a mystical place. Now Toba understands why she has awakened when the sky is still dark behind the floating moon. Toba is the Queen of the Night.

Even in the darkness, Toba can easily tell she is now standing in Bella's room. With all the pictures and drawings and rustling in the wind from the open window, and Bella tossing and turning as if she were dancing in her bed, the room is just as busy at night as Toba's sister is by day.

Bella's dance brings a bounce to Toba's steps as she moves close to the bed. But just as Toba bends to dream the sleeper's dream, Bella turns about sharply, her arm flies up, and nearly hits Toba in the head.

Toba sees right away that to dream Bella's dream, she cannot be so still as she was with Anna. No, the two sisters are very different. The day's light may reveal their likenesses—the same full mouths and red-blond hair—but in the world of the night, Toba can see plainly how different the two really are.

To dream Bella's dream, Toba knows she must be as active as her sister. Quickly, she jumps to her toes and, with the lightest of steps, dances in the silver light flowing through the open window.

Wild winds blowing clouds over the sky. Flocks of black birds wing high and dive. Splendid crowds, turning and spinning in celebration of a grand festival.

Bella's dream is full of loud noises and commotion.

Toba wonders how her sister can sleep with so much in her mind. But Bella would not be Bella if she were to sit still longer than it takes for her to stand up again.

How strange, Toba thinks, *that everything in the dark becomes so clear!*

The Queen of the Night finds this new world the most wonderful place she has ever been. And the best part of all is that this world is hers alone. No one else knows of it, and Toba vows no one ever will. She does one final twirl in Bella's room for the simple reason that it feels so good. As she goes around, a vision comes to her. It is the world of night outside. The smiling moon is playing with the shining clouds, as the stars crown the heads of lovely white swans, floating gently by.

If the world of night is so magical inside the house, Toba thinks, already moving through Bella's doorway, *outside, the night must be most beautiful!*

Half tripping down the stairs in her hurry, Toba catches on to the bannister, hearing her Momma's constant warning, loud in her head, "Toba! One step at a time. You are young yet; the world will wait for you."

Toba stands on the porch and looks out at the gray shadows, the wind blowing through the treetops, freely moving the countless diamond stars about the sky.

"I am the only one awake in the world!" Toba says, and hears a faint, faint echo. "They are

all sleeping, all except for me. The Queen of the Night!"

Before Toba walks down the three steps of the porch to the ground, she takes off her slippers. She would not want them to get soiled. The cold wood beneath her bare feet makes her spring from the second step down onto the moist grass.

Toba turns to look at her house. All the windows are black, and for some reason the whole house looks much smaller. *Maybe everything grows small in the night?* Toba wonders. But not the trees. They look much taller. Toba walks over to one by the fence. It is her favorite tree to sit under in the summer heat. Now, the tree's huge branches shade even the silver beams of the moon, and once beneath its cover, Toba can almost not see herself.

Silently, Toba stands, feeling as if she is in a dream, swimming in a great ocean, swallowed up by the deep black night.

"*OOOOO!*"

Toba jumps.

"*OOO — OOO!*"

The sound is close, but Toba cannot see.

"*OO-OO-OO!*"

Above her head, on a branch, stare two orange eyes.

"*OOOOOOO!*" shrieks the creature, flapping its wings, sending Toba into the air, up the porch, into the house, behind the closed door.

Moments pass before Toba can breathe freely and she realizes that her feet are bare and her slippers are out in the night without her. She decides to leave them there until morning. *There's no good sense in tempting the fates, or an angry owl,* Toba says to herself, *especially in the world of the night.*

Still not prepared to sleep, Toba climbs the stairs to the hallway. Without her slippers, each step makes a sound as though someone is following her.

Toba turns the handle of her parents' bedroom door and walks to the large bed holding her Momma and Papa. This is the first time Toba has ever seen the two sleeping in bed. Back to back, they look much the way Toba would have drawn them in a painting: each prepared to spring up at the first call from one of the three girls, most always Toba herself.

At first there seems to be only one sound rising from the bed, both sleepers breathing in the same breath and out one long, peaceful sigh. But then Toba hears her Momma's singing sigh. It is much the same as the sound she makes while forever waiting for the kettle to boil, or hurrying a late Toba off to school.

Putting her two hands on the sturdy wooden bedpost, Toba closes her eyes and dreams her parents' dream.

A summer evening. All are gathered about the table, heads bowed. The candles' flames flicker and shed a quiet light. Papa stands and sings the prayer over the challah, then cuts one large piece for all to share.

Toba is filled with a terrible, sad feeling. Tears well in her eyes. Her parents' dream is the most beautiful of all dreams. Toba often dreams of her family together. Sometimes she fears that they will be separated. She feels that awful feeling now. Everyone is together, sleeping, dreaming, except for her. Toba is the only one awake in the lonely night.

Toba knows she can wake her parents, she can let out a cry . . . But they look so tired. She can also go back to her room, but what if she cannot sleep? Or, she can crawl into bed with Anna, though sharing a bed like some scared little girl does not seem fitting for the Queen of the Night. So, very simply, Toba curls up on the straw carpet before her parents' bed, and there she sleeps into the following morning, where the sun wakes her.

THE EGG

I

Toba stands still as a frightened doe, her heart fluttering as though it has wings. Alone, nestled in the moist grass, lies an egg, a perfect jewel. The egg is — what Toba's Momma is always searching for — a sign of good fortune.

Oh, how her fingers ache to touch it, weigh its lightness, cup the oval in the soft of her palm and cradle it all the way home to Anna, Bella, Momma, and especially Papa, who keeps a tender place for, as he calls them, "Earth's Angels."

Though her heart tugs her, Toba is careful not to touch the egg. Her Papa has taught her that if you find a bird's egg, or even a baby bird who has fallen from the sky, do not touch it or the momma will not return. Toba keeps this lesson in mind as her curiosity draws her to only a breath away from the speckled shell. If she dared to speak, it would be only words of kindness hushed in a whisper. She wishes the stream, just a few steps ahead, would likewise mind its manners and quiet its babbling.

All the way to the stream, Toba had kept her promise to her Momma, putting "one foot in front of the other," and keeping "in the middle of the crooked road." Her only thought the whole time she walked was how she planned to splash her feet and ankles in the cold current for the first time without someone telling her to be careful of this, and warning her about that. Every other time she'd been to the stream, Toba was led like an animal, locked by the hand, even before they left the front porch, and not freed until back inside. This was true even in winter, when Toba visited the stream with Bella. It was quiet then, the water flowing beneath the blue blanket of ice and white pillows of snow.

Why her Momma finally let her go alone this day, Toba is not sure. At first she had refused, as she had done so many times, saying that Toba was still too young to be so far alone. But in a last effort, Toba told her Momma that she must go alone today, for this was the first day of summer of her eleventh year. And though there was no special meaning in the two dates and their meeting, her Momma softened. (Toba only mentioned the dates because she often noticed the great respect older people had for time and numbers—how they would pause from their serious conversations and ponder the figures.)

In her heart's heart, Toba hopes she will not find the egg's momma, but she knows it would be wrong to carry it off without searching. She looks up at the row of thin, leafy trees whose branches scatter sunlight and shadow over her face, like a veil. But there is no nest. There are many more trees farther down by the stream's edge. A wise Toba unties one of the yellow ribbons from her hair and knots it around a twig to mark the egg's place, so she will not get lost or pass over the tiny thing upon returning from her hunt.

Perhaps the momma is building a new, larger nest for her growing family, or searching for food? *Maybe*, Toba thinks, *the momma has dropped the egg and is right now looking for it, just as I am looking for the momma*. But then Toba remembers her Papa telling her that birds are given sharp sight to see the smallest worm from atop the tallest tree. Toba had asked if the worms had such sight. When her Papa said no, that they were as blind as he, Toba, no lover of the crawling creatures, said, "Poor worms."

Toba's search brings her deep into the forest. There are thousands of colorful birds noisily chirping and hopping from branch to branch. How could she know which is the momma? Could it be that the momma bird is the kind to lay its egg and fly away? Toba's Papa has told her many stories of the cruelties of animals: how momma deer leave their young only weeks after they are born. In the night, while the babies sleep, they sneak away, and in the morning, the little ones find themselves hungry and alone. If they do not find food, they starve. If their new legs do not carry them fast enough, they are food for another. "But deer are the swiftest of all animals," her Papa said, "and their speed protects them."

The harshest of the animal lessons were about birds. Her Papa explained—hugging Toba close when he sensed she had become frightened—that only days after hatching from their shells, the babies are taken in their momma's beak and flown over a field, far from the nest. There, the momma opens her beak and drops her baby. If it does not flap its weak wings and fly, it falls to the ground and is hurt. Some die.

Her Papa had to hold Toba a long time after he told her about the birds. He tried to soothe her, telling her that the birds had no choice. If they did not teach their young to fly this way, they would never learn and they would freeze in winter. "It seems cruel to you now, Toba," he said, "but soon you will understand the kindness." Toba buried her face into her Papa's coat, and swore that she would never understand, never.

Later that day, when Toba was calm, her Papa told her, smiling his sad smile, that this is the way of the world.

"But this isn't even a baby bird!" Toba cries up to the trees, frightening the birds into flight. "This is an egg! No wings to help it fly, no mouth to cry for help, no eyes to see even the *biggest* worm!" Perhaps the momma is not protecting it because someone before Toba found the egg, and the momma smelled the scent of his hands on the shell and left it to be eaten!

Turning to stop the terrible bear whom she is certain is about to make her egg his supper, Toba finds herself in the thick of the forest, surrounded by tall, ugly trees. They twist and tangle, and block the sun. Toba searches for the ribbon, for her egg. Her momma's voice shouts loud in her ears, "If you get lost, don't come running to me!"

Widening her eyes, Toba pushes out her hands and rushes between two gnarled oaks, giant monsters. After only a few swift steps, she is able to swallow down a breath. Ahead is a patch of

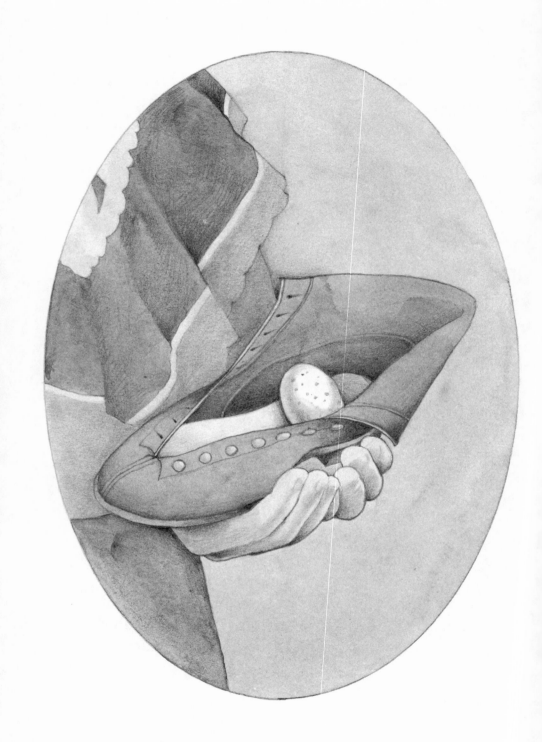

sunlight, then the row of skinny trees. And farther on, the yellow ribbon on the twig, flapping
on the breeze.

II

"What are you doing with your shoe in your
hand?"

Just as Toba had expected, her Momma greets
her at the door with a sour face. "Will you next
wear your skirt on your head?"

And, again just as Toba had thought, her
Momma quiets at the sight of the precious egg,
sleeping on the bed of Toba's cotton stocking.
That, of course, does not excuse such behavior,
Toba agrees, and pouts as she knows is expected.
But all is forgiven as soon as her Momma has
Toba's filthy foot soaking in a basin steaming
with soapy water. Toba's only punishment is to
bear those strong hands gripping and scrubbing
her heel, sole, and each toe, raw and tender.

III

Between meals and chores, Toba places the
wooden bowl—a more proper home than a
shoe—on her windowsill. The days are spent

following the slow arc of the sun. In the morning, the quiet yellow rays slant down on her bedroom's side of the house, by the garden. Those early hours are spent sitting on old planks of wood, beside the upturned soil and green sprouts. When Toba tires of watching and waiting, she tells her egg fairy stories, the ones her Papa used to tell. Only these are of a little princess who finds a magical egg, and how the whole town gathers to look and praise the two of them.

Toward noon, the sun floats higher, over the chimney of the house. The hot glow seems to come right down on the roof and shower the bright warmth everywhere, offering Toba and the egg a great choice of places to sit. Sometimes it is near the broken fence by the twin apple trees, at other times it is beneath the cord on which her Momma hangs the wet clothes. Or they both can be found on the first step of the front porch.

Early evenings, before dinner, when the sun spreads its cool colors through the sky, Mr. Sabine's toolshed is the warmest place. He does not mind if Toba stays there, as long as she promises not to touch his tools. "Especially," he says and points, "not the scythe or the saws or the hoe." The warning is for her own safety. Toba repeats his instructions, showing that she indeed understands his words, and that she must be extra careful now that she is taking care of two. Mr. Sabine seems very impressed, and tells Toba that she is doing something very important. Then he makes a poor joke about being invited to dinner when the egg grows into a plump chicken. But when he sees that she is not laughing, he apologizes and says that he is certain it will be a beautiful bird, especially if it is born with Toba's eyes and nose.

Night time brings the egg back to the windowsill. But should it become cold, Toba has a plan to bring the wooden bowl down to the kitchen, the warmest room. How else can she keep the egg warm? She cannot bring it to bed and hug it close, as she does with her dolls. This egg is alive and very delicate. It seems always to be cautioning in a tiny voice, "Gentle, gentle."

IV

For all Toba's chasing after the sun and storytelling, the egg refuses to move, roll, jiggle, or show any signs of breaking into a wet, twitching life. And so, after four days, she decides to take Bella's advice, and fill her bowl with a fresh bed of grass and bring her egg to Mr. Horowitz.

Of all those in town, Mr. Horowitz is known as the man who knows most about animals and nature. Legend tells of how he found a duck with a broken wing and brought him home, cured him, and the duck has never left.

After lunch and a long, examining stare — the kind all mommas give to their perfect children before presenting them to the eyes of the world — Toba walks her egg over to Mr. Horowitz's farm.

On the way, she prepares questions so she will not seem a braggart who has come to display her prize and beg praise: *What does a baby bird eat its first few days? How often is it fed? Do I have to climb a tree and drop the bird from high up?* Just the thought makes Toba hug the bowl protectively. She would not mind if the bird never flew. She decides she will not mention anything about flying at all.

Toba finds Mr. Horowitz digging long, narrow holes in the black soil near the tomatoes. At first he seems startled upon seeing her, but then he smiles, showing two uneven rows of brown, stumplike teeth. He tells her he is putting in wooden supports to hold up his heavy tomato vines. Then he laughs very loudly, and says that *his* tomatoes are the plumpest, tastiest in all of Poland!

"Now, tell me, what are you hiding behind your back?" Mr. Horowitz asks Toba, who is stunned by the girth of the tomatoes and suddenly wishes she had not brought along her egg at all.

"Come now, Toba, I've never seen you so timid."

Modestly, as if it actually pained her, Toba presents her wooden bowl, hoping he will make as big a fuss as he did over his crop. "Oh!" he says, almost singing, his cracked lips opening wide, his eyes huge. And with his two hands, he takes the bowl and stands. Toba watches him admire her egg, and while his face is hidden by the bowl, she sticks her tongue out at the jealous tomato hiding in shame behind the furry leaves.

"Where did you find this robin's egg, Toba?" Mr. Horowitz asks, in a heavy voice.

"By the stream, near the forest. It was all by itself and I saved it." Toba puts out her hands. She wants her egg back.

"How long ago did you find it?"

"Five days ago." Toba spreads her fingers on her right hands to show five. "It hasn't moved at all."

"Not at all, you say?" asks Mr. Horowitz, sounding much like the doctor, listening and touching for ills. Toba's arms drop to her sides.

"Maybe in the night," she offers, hoping.

Mr. Horowitz grunts, then buries his face in the bowl.

"I never dropped it, or left it alone except when I ate or helped Momma or Papa."

Mr. Horowitz seems deaf. Putting his hand into the bowl, he brings out the egg between his thumb and forefinger, and holds it high to the sun. Toba is shocked silent. The shadow of the egg between his fingers looks like a coin, a stone. Squinting, he shifts his head back and forth, and then brings the egg down to the level of his wide chest, where it disappears into his palm.

Toba feels a crack. Mr. Horowitz opens his hand and studies. He turns his palm to let slide a thick sea of yellow liquid and sharp bits of blue shell.

V

Forced by her Momma and her Papa, who said Mr. Horowitz must have had his reasons, Toba returns to the farm, where she has left the bowl behind. How she hates him! It takes more than a full hour to make the fifteen-minute journey. She will take the bowl from him without a thank you, curse his land, and run away! Maybe, if she is taken with enough anger, she will toss a rock at the evil giant, and he will fall like Goliath.

Toba has prepared herself to see the laughing face of the dybbuk who has burned her, but Mr. Horowitz looks sad. She is ready for his knowing laughter, but his silent, sun-darkened face makes her eyes fill.

"I am glad, Toba," he says, so softly Toba can barely hear. "I called for you to stop, but you ran away."

Toba feels sick, remembering the yellow soup that was her egg.

"The egg was not alive. It was dead when you brought it to me. It was dead when you found it. This is why its momma left it alone."

Toba bows her head. If it was dead, what was that in his hand? What spilled into the earth?

"I broke it in my hand for a reason. It was the same reason you took such good care of the egg. Do you understand?"

Toba shakes her head no. She was *good* to the egg! She had kept it warm, safe. She had tried to bring it to life. *He* was a killer!

"The egg was diseased. If another animal found it and ate it, he, too, would have become diseased. And perhaps a man would have found this animal and brought it home for his family's

food. They, too, would have become ill. By finding that egg and keeping it away from other animals, you have saved their lives. By trying to bring that one egg to life, you, Toba, have saved *many* lives!"

He smiles, showing his chewed, woodlike teeth.

Toba looks up to his brightening face.

"So, you see, what seemed cruel was really kind."

Toba thinks of the birds, dropping their young, and the deer running off in the night.

"Come, I have a surprise for you," he says, his voice now clear and stronger.

Toba does not answer. She is thinking of all the animals she must have saved. And maybe even Mr. Sabine, who wanted to eat her egg. If it hadn't been for her, maybe he, too, would have had to be crushed.

"This is for you, Toba," Mr. Horowitz says, handing her the bowl she had left behind. Toba takes one look and her heart begins fluttering as it had just days before. Those same wings. It is an egg. A beautiful egg. More beautiful than her sick one. It sparkles and shimmers as if it holds a million tiny stars.

"I hope this mends our friendship, Toba," Mr. Horowitz says. "I hope this sweetens your day."

VI

Everyone admires the new egg, while Toba tells them the whole story of how she had saved the entire village from a terrible plague. They are all very proud. Her Papa, upon hearing the story a second time, calls her a tiny messiah. It seems to Toba that her Papa must have known that the egg was ill. That is why he did not get upset when he learned that Mr. Horowitz had crushed it. *Yes, he must have known. It all fits so well*, Toba thinks.

For the next two days, she keeps as close as possible to her fat little prize. And though she does not see it jiggle or roll over, she is sure it is growing larger, and that before the week is over, she will be tending to a chirping life. On the third day, when her Papa calls her to run an errand, Toba promises her egg she will be right back before it opens its shell and becomes a chick, a swan, or even a peacock.

Just a few steps from Mr. Hasner's tailor shop, Toba, weighed down by a bulky load of material, sees Mr. Horowitz. With all her might, she draws a breath, lifts her load and hurries her strides.

"Toba!" Mr. Horowitz calls loudly, dropping

to one knee and taking her bouncing bundle.

Toba is unable to grasp her breath.

"Are you chasing me?" he laughs.

"I am helping my Papa."

"And tell me," he says. "Did you enjoy your egg?"

Toba understands that he is asking if she enjoys caring for the egg. Or perhaps he thinks it is no longer an egg, but now a flying bird.

"Yes," she says, "but it is *still* an egg. Soon — soon — it will be the most beautiful bird in Lenchintz. In all of Poland! Everyone will see. They will know — "

"Toba, *Toba*," Mr. Horowitz says, nearly moaning. "I thought you knew. I thought you understood."

Toba looks at the large man and the dirt stain on his forehead. She thinks he might cry.

"The egg I gave you, it was not a real egg. I thought you knew. It was a sweet. A sugar candy to ease the pain of your sick egg. I thought you knew."

Toba cannot move. *He is lying*, she thinks. *A bad joke. But he is not laughing. This cannot be true. It cannot be.*

"Toba, I am sorry."

Now the dybbuk shows! His green eyes cross! His wooden teeth flame!

VII

"How unfair!" Toba pleads to no one but the flowing stream and the sweet-looking, but oh so evil, candy egg. "This is worse than a deer abandoning her young in the night, worse than a bird dropping her baby from the sky."

Even to her own ears, her words sound harsh, and Toba stops her mouth. But her thoughts continue. At least there is some good to come from dropping the tiny birds; they will learn to fly away and not freeze in the cold. And when the momma deer leaves her little ones, they will learn to run quickly and protect themselves. But she was caring for a *candy*!

Again, Toba falls silent and ponders. For all the harshness, there is kindness in the ways of the animals. She sees this now. But what good is a sweet to her?

Toba looks over the egg she once cradled and sang to. She cannot help but admit that it *is* pretty. And its sweet scent is faint but pleasant. Toba lets her tongue's moist tip touch the shell's sugar coating. She smiles her Papa's sad smile and nods her head, for this is the way of the world.

THE TRAIN RIDE

Toba has her face pressed to the window, which is fogged by her breath. If there is one day she loves above all others, more than her birthday, Chanukah, or any day at all, it is this day each year when her family rides the train to Cracow for the family gathering. It is not that Toba is thrilled with seeing her cousins and aunts and uncles, who all look alike, never call her by the right name, pinch her face, kiss her endlessly and squeeze her belly. What Toba loves so dearly, enough that her heart beats so quickly she fears it will take flight, is the train ride.

The first time Toba can remember riding the train, it seemed to take forever to reach Cracow. But on the last two rides, and even on the one before, the eight hours seemed to go by without a single tick of the conductor's large gold watch.

Anna has said that "scientific advances" have shortened the time. "Quicker wheels, better tracks, and more comfortable cars," she explained to Toba. "All these things help make the train move faster." Toba thought about these many reasons and then told Anna that eight hours seemed just right for the train ride and they should make scientific advances in some other areas where they are needed, "like making garlic taste better."

First awake this morning, there was no need for Toba to endure the same old daily ritual. Every morning it is the same: first, her Momma comes in, singing loud enough to wake the whole next town—six miles away. Next, she opens the window, letting the cold, morning air rush into the perfectly warm bedroom. Even in winter! The cold runs an awful chill up Toba's spine, but she just curls up into herself and pulls her head beneath the blanket, without opening an eye.

It is not long before Toba is called to get out of her night clothes and into her dress for the day, which is always waiting for her on her chair. Finally she is threatened with punishment if she is not downstairs, eating breakfast "and smiling," by the count of ten. "One . . . two . . . " By "three," Toba is up and running, though rarely smiling.

But not this morning. The first up, in her bright red dress, she was at the table, waiting for breakfast, even before it was hot. Toba was so excited, she could have easily skipped breakfast and gone on right to the depot.

Though the train station is not far from the Cohens' home, they had to ride in the carriage this morning because of all they had to carry. Toba's Papa sewed a kerchief for every woman in the family and a little baby one for Zeitel, the newest member of the family, born not three months ago.

So, when the sun was just rising to wake the world, a busy Toba helped load Mr. Gaston's newly painted wagon for their bumpy, winding ride to the train. This trip, too, Toba enjoyed, the whole time remembering just the sounds the engine of the train makes as it pulls into the station, roaring and whistling, and blowing great clouds of blue steam proudly for all to see. And then, just before the train slows to a stop, there is a sudden wind which fills all the women's skirts and snatches at the men's hats, followed by a piercing screech of the metal wheels which hurts everyone's ears and forces their hands to their heads. Oh, yes, Toba remembers it all, even the coal-covered hands and face of the engineer.

This year Toba was happy not to find any scientific advances. The same shining, black engine, pounding and churning like a wild beast, the same great clouds of blue steam, the same colorful crowd of laughing people, waiting at the platform, and that very same wonderful, painful screech—fulfill all of Toba's high hopes.

Once in their compartment, with the soft, red leather seats, each bearing up to the test of Toba's firm bounce, the five passengers removed their overcoats and put away their baggage in the wooden drawer above their heads. Toba quickly took the seat by the window and prepared to remain there, kneeling, face against the glass, for the full eight hours, eyes wide every minute of the trip.

"Tickets. Tickets, please," the conductor calls, making Toba reluctantly turn her head. But when she sees the pained expression on her Momma's face as she reaches into her bag for the expensive tickets, Toba quickly turns away.

The whistle shouts three short times and then lets out a long cry. There is a violent jerk, which nearly sends Toba on her back, but does not touch the smile on her face. "All aboard. Next stop Lublin," the conductor calls. "Lublin, next stop. All aboard."

And slowly, as if they are running up a too steep hill, slowly the wheels begin to move,

creaking loudly. The crowd of people on the platform waves and calls out good wishes. And soon the train is out of the station, moving effortlessly, as if on air. From the window, all they pass — the green and brown land of autumn, the naked trees and squat homes — mixes and blends together, reminding Toba of her paintings when she uses too much water.

While her Momma sews the trim on still another sweater for Zeitel, and her Papa hums some familiar songs, and Bella and Anna read their schoolbooks, Toba watches the world rush by with the speed of dancers, dressed in colorful costumes. Even the sky seems to be racing the train, leaving the poor birds, flapping their weak wings, to fall far behind.

"Oh, dear. Oh, no!" A loud sobbing fills the Cohens' compartment and again forces Toba's face from her faint reflection in the glass.

"What will I do!" a very fat woman, wearing a hat with a veil, wheezes as she crowds into the small compartment.

"There is a problem?" Toba's Momma asks, putting down her sewing.

"Alex. My Alex is gone! Lost. We boarded here just a while ago in Lublin on our way to Slenick, and just when I took my seat, he was not behind me. Oh!" The woman's great weight and shaking makes everyone move about, uncomfortably.

"Maybe he never boarded the train?" Anna says.

"Oooh," the woman moans, her thick legs weakening.

"Or perhaps he is walking about the train, lost," Bella offers.

Again, the woman nearly swoons.

"Oh, I do hope so," she says, sniffing at her lace handkerchief. "I truly do hope so. Please, if you see a little red-headed boy, tell him his aunt Ida is worried. Terribly worried." And turning about as slowly as it is possible to turn, the woman struggles from the compartment, leaving behind a heavy sense of grief and a trail of "Ooohs."

This happens each year, Toba tells herself — not that a little boy gets lost, but that, on and off, between each stop, people come into their compartment, say a little something, and then turn, never to be seen again.

"I hope she finds her boy safe," Momma says, and all follow with a nod. Toba hears her Papa breathe a prayer.

She wonders how, after passing so many towns — Lenchintz, Tem, Gez — there can possibly be four more hours to travel before they reach Cracow. Momma spreads a tablecloth over everyone's knees and from a wooden basket she takes out lunch. It makes Toba's head spin to think that so much food can fit into the basket. There are meats, potatoes, cabbage, bread, fruits, and a jug of cool water.

"Smells fine. Yes, I say. Something has the distinct aroma of well-cooked beef, tender vegetables, and ripened fruit." A tall, bony man, with his tie undone about his neck, bends and sways into the compartment. His eyes seem as if he has a cold. "But, eat. Enjoy. Please do not stop your feast on my account." He leans in so far that he fills the compartment with a sweet smell of something familiar. Toba takes a moment to close her eyes, and draws a deep breath.

"Wine!" she says loudly, having sniffed out just what the scent is. Bella puts her finger to her lips to hush her little sister.

Momma sternly offers him a slice of meat, a piece of bread, and a wedge of a small, green pear.

The man swallows this down so quickly, Toba wonders if he has ever eaten before. He then bows deeply, almost tumbling over into Anna's lap, and after many too many *thank you*'s and *bless you*'s, he walks into the next compartment, where he is heard again to comment on the flavorful aroma, this time of a "succulent stew."

Toba finishes her lunch and turns to admire the endless painting of the now dark rain clouds, hanging just above the silken waves of wheat.

The train moves so smoothly, it is as if she is dreaming. She hopes she never wakes.

"True. Very true," says a strange, deep voice. "Each time I travel, I am reminded of the Book of Jonah, and this one man's miraculous voyage."

Toba turns about to see a black-bearded man wearing a black hat and long coat. He must have sat down next to her Papa while she was imagining herself flying over the hills of Ozrcough.

"What an experience to be transported in the mouth of a leviathan!" The man—Toba thinks he must be a rabbi—repeats loudly, "What an experience!"

She is glad for her Papa that he has someone to talk with, although she knows well he will mostly listen.

"Yes, here is a picture of my husband." Toba turns the other way. How did this woman find her way into the compartment? Toba must have been far off not to notice how crowded and noisy it has become.

"He is leaving for America," the woman tells Anna, while Bella looks over the photograph. "I must stay behind and have my baby. Then he will call for me to join him in our beautiful new home in America."

America, America, Toba repeats to herself, thinking of how everyone, lately, has been talking of this land which holds so much promise.

Toba marvels at the two worlds about her. One so silent and grand, rushing by but changing only slightly. And the other, in their tiny compartment; here crowded together, are these people from all over, going all over, thinking different thoughts, dreaming such different dreams.

"Cracow! Next stop Cracow!"

It is night. Toba has seen the sun rise and then set, only to be overcome by the black night. As she helps her Momma pack up all their belongings, a boy peeks his head into their compartment. His red hair is full and wavy.

Everyone lets out a sigh of relief.

The train slows to a crawl and then a full stop, with a loud screech. But Toba does not raise her hands to her head. Closing her eyes, she lets the piercing sound fill her ears, her head, her whole body. Soon the noise fades. Toba stands. Through the window she can see her many relatives, smiling and waving.

PAINTING

Toba bends over the white paper. It is difficult to tell what will happen next. Will she stick out her tongue and taste the whiteness? Will she let out a great breath to slowly draw in the pure scent? Or, finally, will she take her brush from the glass of water, dip its tip into a colored block, and paint?

When Toba is painting, ideas come to her that make no sense. There are moments when she thinks she does not need her eyes to see colors; the very reds, blues, greens of her mind come through the tips of her fingers. Other times, after she has mixed two or three colors to create another, she likes to feel the new, slippery liquid run over her palm, filling the narrow cracks.

Once, a color she made was so much like the crystal blue of lake water, she could not help but put her tongue to it.

"Toba, your tongue is blue!" cried her Momma, whose face turned pale.

Toba could not admit what a fool she had

been; instead, she make a joke. "My tongue is blue," she said, "because I climbed a tree and tasted the sky."

Colors are what Toba likes most about painting. As long as the colors are true, the lines that form a face can be all wrong, and that face can still be handsome, or pretty, or ugly if that's how the person was born.

Toba dips her paintbrush into the glass of water, and watches the yellow—the color of the sun—drift off and spread. It is a fine sun, floating high over clouds of white. Full, green trees are dotted with red apples and brown pears. Blackbirds fly by, chirping merrily.

A thick layer of sunken colors that have washed from the silky hairs of Toba's brush lay heavy on the glass's bottom. With a quick stir, those colors swim up and whirl, and it is easy to tell the red from the yellow, the blue from the green. Toba mixes and studies the many colors that she does not have in her set of five paint wells: the violet of the waving flowers in the fields, the silver of the lake when the sun slants playfully, the gray of early winter mornings.

The man in Toba's painting sits in a sturdy wooden chair, his arms spread wide. Except for the face, Toba leaves the hands for last. The face is the very hardest, and her least favorite to

paint. She has ruined many good paintings with a too-crooked nose or a fat, sloppy mouth, or eyes that cross.

The birds ride the breezes, their beaks sharp and open for singing. Pears and apples ripen with juice and taste, and hang heavy from the trees' limbs. And now, even the man's hands, as Toba touches their backs with wandering curls of gray, become tender.

Toba dries the brush on a rag, dips its tip into the well of shining yellow, and lightly pecks his two palms. Quicker than thought, she puts the brush back into the water, spins, wipes the tip dry, and places the bristles first into the black and then into the blue wells. This is how she makes brown. With a few tiny strokes, the hands are filled with seeds and crusts of bread for the hungry birds.

Toba looks at the man's empty face, and quickly turns away. She finds a place for another bird, and lands him on the man's square shoulder. This bird is larger than the others, and Toba gives him a proud red breast, and then longer claws and extra feathers.

"Careful, careful," Toba warns herself. Cluttering her paintings is a constant problem. She knows that too much can ruin her work, but often the joy of drawing lines, placing colors, filling blank space with everything in a day, becomes stronger than her will, and what was once a quiet stream is soon a violent river, overflowing with fish, fallen trees, and ships. A child playing is soon joined by animals, friends, and Toba finds herself involved in a family portrait, complete with uncles, aunts, cousins, and pets. It seems sinful to leave anything out, but Toba has learned it is worse to crowd her paintings. Each flower must have its rain and sun, each bird needs its branch and food.

Toba looks at the face of the man, knowing she cannot put off the features forever. She coaxes herself with the thought that the birds cannot eat unless the man knows they are there, and without ears he cannot hear them singing for their supper.

Carefully, Toba touches the brush's tip to the black and blue wells, and lightly leads the fine hair in a tiny, swirling motion on the right, then the left side of the man's long, oval head. She touches a watery red to thin them, and the ears are done.

"Now he can hear how sweetly the birds sing! But he hasn't a mouth. He cannot even join in their songs."

Gently, she places an open, joyful mouth on the man. "How he sings! Now the birds flock about him, and feast."

The nose, since he is a man, is not so difficult as it would have been if he were a boy, or a woman, without a beard to disguise the faults. With sharp, careless strokes, he is able to smell the fragrance of the blooming fields and the trees' fruit. Toba draws tight, gray curls for his head and beard, which fills out his face and lies long on his chest. The proud, red-breasted bird's beak becomes tangled in the bearlike fur.

Now, all that is left to complete this perfect picture are the eyes. Toba draws the brush from the wells of paint, and decides to rest. Absently, she stirs the murky mixture on the glass's bottom. Like dancers, the colors, one by one, sweep up, then, in pairs, twirl and spin. The fragile brown of leaves in autumn, the soft yellow of her sisters' hair, the dusty black of coal, then the glint of a silver star. "Colors are magic," Toba hears, as if the words never passed her lips, but were carried to her ears on a breeze.

The fear of touching sight to the man blends with the vivid colors in Toba's mind, painting a picture for her. A painting of her Papa, sitting in his dark room, blind.

The man in her painting is, as are most of the men she draws, Toba's Papa. When he first lost his sight, Toba could not bear to look at him. He was not suddenly ugly or scarred; she could not look at him because he could not look at her. *She* was able to look way up into the sky and see the future, the dark clouds over the mountains, fat with rain, the last glimmer of day that welcomes the night, while her Papa could not see the needle in his own hands, the chair in which he sits, the prayers he recites.

She had tried making a bargain with God. She would not be able to see so far if her Papa could just see what was close to him. A fair deal, she thought.

It was her Papa who had first told her that eyes were not needed to see. That was when he first lost his sight, and she had cried.

"I can see your shining face, Tobala," he would hush, his fingers tracing over her cheeks, her chin, stroking her hair. "I can see your smile and your dirty knees and your eyes glowing like flames."

At first, she thought her Papa was just sooth-ing her—a story to chase away the bad dream. But now that she is a painter, Toba understands. When she paints her pictures, she, too, can see special colors, more brilliant than the summer sky, shinier than a new kopek, richer than the darkest soil. This, Toba knows, is not one of her strange thoughts. This is the truth. Something only she and her Papa know. And even though he will never see her paintings, Toba is sure that in his head there are the most beautiful pictures. She, herself, puts them there when she describes her paintings: a frightened doe tricked into flight; the fallen trees uprooted by an awful wind; just the way Momma bends to stoke the stove. Toba can see in her Papa's slow nods, his small, waving hands, that he sees it all clearly, perfectly.

Stirring the wondrous water, Toba studies her painting. The birds are in flight, singing and eating. The trees are blessed with tempting fruit, and the flowers are many and straining for the sun's favor. The man listens, and joins the birds' song. He tastes the sweetness of the trees by their heavenly scent. And when his hands are empty of seeds and crumbs, he reaches into his coat pockets for more.

BARGAIN

Toba is taking her time walking the street this cool day. Her Momma has just stepped into the grocer's for sugar, flour, and a small list of other foods. Already they have been to the butcher, where they bought two pounds of chicken, a half pound of lamb, three small fish, but Momma has refused to take home even a thin slice of the lox.

"It's green!" she said, ignoring the scowl on Mr. Ketchum's face. "Would you put this on *your* family's table?"

At the bakery, Momma has bought one dozen sweet rolls, picking each, one by one, from the basket while they were still warm and sticky. The bakery is Toba's favorite shop for two reasons. The first is the heavenly scent that makes her dizzy with delight. The second is Mrs. Newman, who always gives her a piece from a broken cookie.

"Try the raisin bread today," Mr. Newman told Toba's Momma, who simply said no with the wave of her hand. "Take a loaf of the bread, Yetta. It's very good. We put honey in."

"I make my own bread, also with honey *and* a half pound of walnuts. And I don't charge myself too much, either," Momma told the baker, who shrugged and walked off into the back room where the great ovens stand like dark monsters.

Before they left, Momma paused over the wheat cakes, Papa's favorites. She took two. "They are expensive," she sighs to Toba each time she buys them, "but your Papa enjoys them so."

Toba understands the seriousness of each purchase in each shop. Momma is never so severe as she is when she is shopping. But in spite of her grave features, her brow wrinkling deeply over the size of two cabbages, her eyes narrowing on the blemish on a pear, her tongue rolling over a sample of a sweet from the confectioner, Toba can sense her Momma's strong pleasure in each act.

Toba has learned that making decisions is not so easy. One cannot simply point at one item or the other and say, "That one." You have to think, to question, to weigh, and then—after all this is done—to make a good purchase you have to bargain. "This is a price or are you telling me the year?" her Momma is often heard to ask.

"There she is! Our favorite customer!"

Toba stops in the street.

"What is your pleasure, this breezy day, young lady? Perhaps you fancy an almost new egg holder?"

The two men who call after Toba are peddlers. It was at their crooked hands that she learned a painful lesson about poor purchases.

The peddlers do not live in the village, but each morning they appear with their cart to sell their wares. "Junk," her Momma says.

The men continue to call, but Toba does not respond. She turns her back on the thieves who forced her to spend her entire month's savings — two kopeks — on a bread basket with a small tear in the weave.

"Worth twice the price," said the peddler with the worn blue cap, holding up the basket and trying to cover the hole with his thumb.

"Maybe we are just giving it away for so little?" questioned the other, whose lips always carried the remains of his last meal about them. "I think this young lady is charming us into letting her steal this lovely bread basket for such a pittance."

"She should be ashamed," they agreed.

Toba liked the bread basket well enough, but

she knew that once she brought it home, she would not place bread or cakes or any baked goods in it. She would use this as a bed for her dearest and now badly damaged doll. Since Toba stopped paying attention to him, poor Vicka had been sleeping in her closet, beneath her shoes. Toba thought this basket would make a comfortable bed for Vicka's old age.

But then, she pondered the price. Spending two kopeks would mean she would have to sacrifice sweets from the confectionery, or a new ribbon from the dress shop, and she could not save her half kopek this week, as is her custom. *But then, I'm not saving for anything special, anyway*, Toba coaxed herself. *So who will know the difference?*

But just as she was about to pay the price, she remembered it was September and Bella's birthday was not far off, and that was always too quickly followed by Momma's. "I will need the money for their presents," Toba said nodding at her foresight.

"Yes, I think you are right, my partner," said the capped peddler. "This little fox is trying to *steal* this precious basket from right under our noses!"

"Like I said," the messy one responded, "two kopeks is too little for such a basket as this. Too little, I say."

Toba's mind raced. If she didn't decide quickly between a bed for her poor old doll, who gave her such joy when she was lonely, or the presents for Bella and Momma, who well deserved the best, the peddlers would take back their offer.

"Well, what will it be, my young princess?" one or the other asked. "Will you take it from us at two kopeks or will we sell this lovely basket for five kopeks to another?

He lay the basket in Toba's hand as if it were a baby. She held it gently and turned it about in her hands. The hole was so small, and she could surely place a soft piece of Papa's scrap material to make Vicka a warm mattress . . .

"Hurry! Hurry!" said the one with crumbs falling from his lips.

"Yes or no?" the other said, straightening his cap.

Toba now held the basket in one hand and two smooth coins in the other. In an instant, she closed her eyes tight and one hand was empty.

"A wise shopper you are, my darling."

"Yes, but with your good eye for value. No wonder we are paupers."

Toba stood in the street busy with people passing by, carriages moving along. The men were quickly off, selling a similar basket to a woman while her baby cried in her husband's arms.

"What have you there?" Toba's Momma had come out from one of the stores, walking quickly.

"A basket," Toba said, proudly. "I bought this basket from the peddlers."

"Did you?" her Momma said, surprised. She took the piece into her hands and quickly found the hole. "You bought a basket with a hole in it? For this you *paid*?"

Toba just nodded. She could not get out the words to explain her plan for her home-less doll.

"You spent a kopek on this piece of junk!" Momma's voice rose.

Toba looked down and thought, *What will she think when I tell her I bought this piece of junk for two kopeks?*

"Come, come, my little bargain shopper!" one peddler calls again, though Toba does not turn. She can only think about the basket they sold her for too much money, the basket which was too small for Vicka. No matter how she placed him, his feet stuck out over the side, and his head hung from the edge.

"Why are you treating us this way, little princess?"

"Is there something we have done to offend you?"

Toba turns to tell them to their faces. "That basket you sold me was junk!"

"Junk?" the sloppy one says, wiping syrup from his chin.

"That is what the lady said—*junk*!" the other repeats.

"Well, to some that basket is junk, I suppose," says the first. "To another, that same basket you bought for four kopeks is a treasure."

"*Two* kopeks!" Toba corrects, sternly.

"Only *two* kopeks? Is that all?" he says. "Why, we sold that same one for ten!"

"Ha!" says Toba, and turns her back.

"You don't believe us, little lady? Well, then, I will prove to you this is true."

Toba turns to see the proof. High in the hands of the blue-capped peddler shines a polished brass dish with many small designs carved into its sides and bottom.

Toba gasps.

"Beautiful," croons the poor eater.

"A work of true art," says the other, and places the dish in Toba's waiting hands.

"Now, tell us, what do you think this treasure is worth?"

Toba takes her time. She examines every inch, every design, the inside and outside. This time she will not be fooled.

"Five kopeks," she says. "No more."

"Five!" laughs one.

"You mean *twenty*-five!" says his partner.

"Maybe six." Toba softens as she discovers a lovely tree etched into the top.

"This piece is worth thirty kopeks, if not more," the capped one says, and quickly snatches it from Toba's hands.

"But—" he adds, and pauses sharply. "We will let you take this home and keep it for less . . . *Much less*. Only because you are so unhappy with your basket, and because you have the prettiest eyes we have ever seen."

"Precious stones," his friend agrees.

Toba looks at the brass dish, shining in the sun. It is very special, something her Momma would be pleased to receive on her birthday. A good deal would surely make up for the extra kopeks she wasted on the basket, now used to hold house dustrags.

"How much?" Toba asks, pretending, like her Momma, that she has no interest in the item.

"For you, we will bleed ourselves, and give up this wonderful treasure for ten kopeks."

"Two," Toba says, and means it.

"Five," says the mouth with the syrup.

"Three," Toba says.

"Four," whines the hatted one.

"Or maybe it is only worth two?" Toba ponders, aloud.

"Three! Take it for three," says the one with the hat, as if Toba has stuck him with a pin. "And remember, you are starving us."

Toba pulls out from her pocket the three coins, and just hopes that she has not again been these two men's fool.

"What have you there, Toba?" Momma appears from the grocer's with a bag of goods and a knowing voice.

"A dish, Momma." Toba holds it up for inspection. "A very, *very* bea-u-ti-ful dish."

"Very, *very* beautiful, is it?" her Momma questions, as she hands Toba the sugar and looks the dish over. "How much did you pay?"

"How much is it worth?" Toba answers the question with a question, another trick learned at the hand of her Momma.

"How much?" her Momma asks herself, and gives it another turn in her hands. "Eight kopeks . . . " Toba's heart leaps. " . . . is too much." Then sinks.

"This is worth . . . seven kopeks," her Momma decides. "How much more did you give those robbers?"

"Seven kopeks?" Toba smiles. "For seven kopeks, I would be a fool to sell you this fine dish. But, if you like, you may make me a more reasonable offer, and I will think it over."

"Such a businesswoman!" Momma says, impressed, and walks on, examining the dish and weighing its worth.

Toba knows she will not sell the piece. It is too valuable. She will make it a gift to her Momma on her birthday. Until then, she herself will enjoy and polish it every day.

. . . But then again, she thinks if a fair price is offered, who is she to argue . . .

THE WEDDING

Huddled tight, Toba closes her eyes and becomes a fat ball of yarn, a speck of dust, a forgotten spoon, yellowed and bent. With all the hollering and running about the house — Anna in the kitchen, talking with great movements of her hands, Bella bouncing up and down the staircase as if she has lost her mind, Momma everywhere at once and never in the right place, and even Papa, his foot tapping to some silent rhythm in his workroom — Toba thinks there might be some peace, some tiny space for her to push into, far from the world, in her clothes closet.

Yesterday, for one perfect moment, everything stopped. The air stilled, the wooden floors rested, doors shut and stayed, and Toba was certain she heard the earth sigh. But just as suddenly, there was a creak, perhaps a mouse scampering across the porch, or a dried leaf scratching its back against the roof — who knows? But that was all it took, one creak, and the world once again began going crazy.

Anna, the oldest of the three sisters, is getting married to skinny Benjamin, the dairy farmer's son. The wedding comes as a surprise to no one. This match was made even before Toba could speak.

Benjamin is kind to Toba, and she thinks that he is handsome, though he smells like bad cheese. Toba also thinks that Anna should not marry him. Anna should marry Simon, the silversmith, who tells poor jokes and has hands smooth as glass. If anyone should marry Benjamin, it is Bella. Toba has good reasons for these pairings, but whenever she tries to explain them the words become tangled and make no sense at all.

So, it is just as well that when she tried to tell her Momma of these mismatches, Momma hadn't heard. She was too busy sewing or cooking or praying or in between one and the other.

"Toba! Toba!"

Toba hears the calls, but she is now a stone, kicked into the house from the road, and rolled all the way up to her closet where she rests on a scrap of cloth used to fill a drafty hole. For a stone, this is a fine bed.

"Toba! Please! *Toba*!"

Stones do not talk. They do not hear, either.

Or do they? Toba the stone can hear. Let them prove otherwise!

There are hushed voices followed by hurried steps, some far, others approaching. *"Toba!"* Anna calls, probably waving her hands about her head like wild birds. "Toba, help us!"

She knows what they mean: fold the laundry, serve tea to chatty guests, walk a bundle over to a neighbor. The list has been endless these days. Toba has been asked to "help" with everything. With everyone so busy, why is it that *she* is doing all the work?

"Maybe she's outside," Bella calls from what sounds like the staircase.

Toba has been trying but cannot seem to understand what it is about Anna's wedding that is making Bella run up and down the stairs so.

"I think she is by Papa," answers Momma, her voice loud and breathy, probably because she is thinking about five things at once. No— Toba counts again, and finds her Momma with at least a half dozen thoughts crowding her head and more just waiting to get in. Toba has become a magic stone, clear as rain, the kind of stone she has heard witches use to see the future and read others' thoughts.

"Where can she be?"

Toba knows she should answer. It is not right

for everyone to be thinking only of her. But, then, they are not thinking of her, really. They are thinking about Toba the child, the youngest daughter, the littlest sister, the one who can never manage to eat as much as she leaves on her plate. Right now, she is Toba the stone: small, hard, the kind that shines even in the dark, as if it keeps a tiny lantern all its own in its center—just like the jewel Benjamin has placed upon Anna's finger.

"*Beautiful*," everyone hushed when they saw the ring. "*Beautiful*."

That's one more thing about the wedding Toba cannot make sense of. Everything is beautiful! Could it be a spell? Toba sees no changes. Ever since the preparations began, all she hears is, "Anna is beautiful. Momma is beautiful." Beautiful is a dishrag, a breeze, even bearded Benjamin. If someone asks about the dinner meat, Toba already knows the answer will be "Beautiful."

"Toba! Toba! *Toba*!"

Such hollering! Such noise! Even if it were proved that a stone cannot hear, in this house the stone would turn over onto its belly and roll away, just from the great winds of their voices! And it would all be the fault of this wedding.

Anna, like that stone, will be leaving because

of the wedding. Toba has seen the house where Anna will live with Benjamin and their goats. It is small and cold and Toba thinks Anna would be happier staying where she is. But because of the wedding she is forced away.

Toba doesn't believe Anna, or anyone, when they look at that other house and say, "Beautiful." She would tell them what it really is, but they have not asked. They have not asked her about any of the wedding plans, except Bella, who made everyone laugh when she asked Toba if she could wait to be a bride.

"Yes, I can wait!" the stone shouts.

A silence follows. Footsteps quickly climb the stairs, each loud and strong, coming from far and stopping just outside the closet door.

Toba opens her eyes and can see even in the dark that she is not a stone. Yesterday, when everything quieted, she could hear the earth breathe peacefully. Now she hears the silence growl.

Pushing away the clothes, Toba turns the knob of the door and walks into the crowded room. Anna stands with her hands heavy on her hips. Bella is not moving up or down. Momma is clearly in one place, thinking one thought.

In the stillness, Toba waits for someone to say she is beautiful.

FAMILY PORTRAIT

If Toba has to keep smiling for even one more instant, surely her lips will fall off, followed by every one of her teeth. Bella has her heavy hand pressed on her little sister's shoulder, her fingers moving restlessly. Momma is unusually still, and seems nervous, as if she wants very much to say something, but is holding in her words under great pain. Anna is on Momma's right side, breathing deeply, trying to keep her bangs from falling into her eyes. Beside her, dressed in a new suit, but still smelling like goat's cheese, is Benjamin—the newest family member. Papa sits in the center of them all, still as a statue, looking more handsome than Toba can believe.

"One more minute," the photographer promises once again. Either he is a terrible liar or he is unable to tell time. "Please. Everyone be still. This will be a beautiful treasure for always."

The moment after the powder flashes, Toba will scream, jump up and down, make faces and roll all over the floor. Even though she is wear-

ing a new white dress — she does not give a care.

The photographer moves about like a mad person, charging here to touch Anna's bangs, then back under the black tent behind his camera, then up again, straightening Bella's shoulders, twisting Momma's head. Toba must point her toes just so. Papa is told to run his hand through his beard, "to give the hair a riverlike current."

Not only will she roll about the floor in her new white dress, but Toba will make certain to find her way out the door into the thickest puddle of mud and cover herself completely.

"Yes, yes. I believe we have the poses correct," the photographer says, and once again Toba believes him as she has believed him the countless other times he has said the same words.

He crouches low beneath the black curtain and, miraculous as it seems, he does not pop his head out to comment, or jump up as if someone has pinched him.

"Take a deep breath."

Toba sucks down a musty mouthful. She can already feel the cool mud, slippery and rich. She smiles as bright as can be.

There comes an endless silence, as if the clocks of all the world have stopped. There is flash of blinding light. Then, darkness.